# Spooky Sports Day

WITHDRAWN

*With special thanks to Jim Collins*

First published in Great Britain in 2012 by Buster Books,
an imprint of Michael O'Mara Books Limited,
9 Lion Yard, Tremadoc Road, London SW4 7NQ

www.busterbooks.co.uk
www.monstrousmaud.co.uk

Series created by Working Partners Limited
Text copyright © Working Partners Limited 2012

Cover design by Nicola Theobald

Illustration copyright © Buster Books 2012
Illustrations by Sarah Horne

All rights reserved. No part of this publication may be reproduced, stored in a retrieval system, or transmitted by any means, without the prior permission in writing of the publisher, nor be otherwise circulated in any form of binding or cover other than that in which it is published and without a similar condition including this condition being imposed on the subsequent purchaser.

A CIP catalogue record for this book is available
from the British Library.

ISBN: 978-1-78055-073-2 in paperback print format
ISBN: 978-1-78055-081-7 in Epub format
ISBN: 978-1-78055-080-0 in Mobipocket format

1 3 5 7 9 10 8 6 4 2

Papers used by Michael O'Mara Books are natural, recyclable products made from wood grown in sustainable forests. The manufacturing processes conform to the environmental regulations of the country of origin.

Printed and bound in March 2012 by CPI Group (UK) Ltd,
108 Beddington Lane, Croydon, CR0 4YY, United Kingdom.

# Spooky Sports Day

A. B. Saddlewick

BUSTER

# Chapter One

Maud's pet rat Quentin peeked up out of the top pocket of her polo shirt. When he saw Penelope, he squeaked with fear and dived back down again.

Maud heard sniggering behind her, and turned to see her least favourite classmate. Poisonous Penelope was a witch with a ragged black dress, a pointy hat and long purple hair, and she never missed an opportunity to bully Paprika and Maud.

"Come on, Paprika! It's sports day soon," shouted Maud. "You can do it. I know you can!"

Paprika took a run up and flung the metal

helmet towards the net. It bounced once, then twice …

… and went a full broomstick wide of the goalposts, landing in the long grass beyond the playing field.

"Bad show!" shouted the detached head of their PE teacher, Mr Galahad, from inside the helmet. At the side of the playing field, his armour-clad body was standing with its arms folded.

Maud sighed and went over to find Mr Galahad's head in the grass.

"Over here, child," he called, his bushy moustache twitching.

"Found you, Sir," said Maud. She picked the head up and tossed it back to Paprika, but it slipped through his fingers and flew all the way to the other side of the playing field.

"Ouch!" roared the teacher's head, as it rolled away. "Pay attention, boy! This helmet isn't padded, you know!"

"Sorry," mumbled Paprika, looking round at his classmates and wincing.

Class 3B had been playing Monsterball against Class 2C for half an hour, and Paprika hadn't managed to score a single goal. No matter how close he stood to the net, actually throwing the head into it seemed to be beyond him.

Maud felt sorry for Paprika. Because he was a vampire, everyone expected him to be strong and fast, and they couldn't understand why he was terrible at PE. But Maud had recently discovered that Paprika was actually half-vampire and half-human. And it certainly wasn't the vampire side he took after when it came to playing sports.

Paprika fixed his gaze on the net, frowning hard, and threw the head again. This time it only got halfway there before it hit something and fell to the ground. Paprika looked away from his teammates, blushing with shame.

"Ow," shouted a voice from where the helmet

had fallen. It was Isabel, Maud's invisible classmate. "Stop throwing things at me! It's bad enough that no one ever passes the helmet to me without having it lobbed at my head."

"He didn't mean it," said Maud. Paprika was her best friend at Rotwood School, and she didn't like it when the other pupils were rude to him.

"Stop making excuses for him," said Penelope. "He's about as much use as a chocolate cauldron. It's only four days until sports day and, thanks to him, our class is going to come last."

"He might not be great at Monsterball," said Maud, remembering something that had happened the week before, "but at least he isn't a scaredy-cat who jumps out of his skin at the sight of a tiny doll."

"Any real monster would have been scared of that hideous thing," said Penelope, narrowing her eyes. "If you ask me, it's pretty funny that you weren't."

Maud shifted around uncomfortably. The truth was that she was the only pupil at Rotwood who wasn't a real monster. Penelope was a witch, Paprika was a half-vampire and Invisible Isabel was … well, invisible. But Maud was just an ordinary human girl. She'd been transferred to Rotwood the week before and she'd pretended to be a 'Tutu' monster so she could stay. Rotwood was so much better than her old school, Primrose Towers.

"Let's get on with the game," shouted Mr Galahad. His head had landed near an ants' nest and his eyes were darting around nervously as a trail of the insects marched towards his nostrils.

While Maud's werewolf friend Wilf returned the head to the middle of the playing field, Maud reached into the top pocket of her polo shirt and stroked Quentin. Her pet rat was trembling from all the running about she had been doing. Poor Quentin was always nervous about something.

"It's all right," she said. "There's nothing to worry about."

"Play on!" boomed the voice from Mr Galahad's helmet.

Maud rushed forward and picked up the helmet. She made a solid run up the field, dodging a mummy and a demon on the way, and she was about to try for goal when Bartholomew Bones the skeleton boy lunged at her. Maud threw Mr Galahad's head to the only teammate who was nearby.

Unfortunately, that teammate was Paprika.

Paprika dashed towards the helmet with his hands out. Maud held her breath. This time, it looked as though he might actually catch it. But just as the tips of his fingers were about to make contact with the spinning head, he tripped over his feet and went crashing down to the ground.

"Enjoy your trip," shouted Penelope.

Mr Galahad's head went rolling back into a muddy puddle.

"Someone tied my laces together!" shouted Paprika.

"Stop making excuses and get me out of this filthy soup," gurgled Mr Galahad.

Maud could see Penelope sniggering to herself at the side of the playing field. She knew what must have happened – Penelope had cast a spell to knot Paprika's laces together. What a bully! It was bad enough when Penelope teased her friend, but casting a spell on him was the last straw. Time to give Penelope a taste of her own medicine.

There wasn't much a monster feared. Spiders, graveyards and rats were useless, but Maud had recently found out that monsters were terrified of pink, cute stuff like dolls or teddy bears. She knew one thing that was sure to scare Penelope.

As the witch went running to pick up their teacher's head, Maud shouted out, "Behind you! Bunny rabbit!"

Penelope's eyes went wide, and she turned to look, crashing into Oscar, the headless boy, so that they both fell flat on the ground. When she glanced up at Maud, her face was almost as purple as her hair. Without even getting up, she stretched out her arm and muttered under her breath again.

Maud ducked, but she was too late. It felt like a huge hand had smacked into her stomach and she hit the ground so hard it knocked the wind out of her.

Maud scrambled to her feet and charged at Penelope. All the pupils from 3B and 2C were crowding round, chanting, "Duel! Duel! Duel!"

Just as Maud was getting close to the witch, a large bulk moved in between them. She skidded to a halt. It was the body of Mr Galahad. One hand was on his hip, while the other held out his soggy head, his moustache dripping with puddle water.

"That's quite enough, young ladies. This silly nonsense is the last thing we need," shouted Mr Galahad. "Both of you go and see the Head right now!"

Penelope's face went very pale indeed.

# Chapter Two

Maud sat on a rickety wooden chair outside the Head's office, fiddling with the hem of her skirt.

Penelope was on the chair next to her with her hands in her lap, and Maud noticed they were trembling with fear. It wasn't surprising. All the pupils at Rotwood were terrified of the Head, and the strange yowling sounds coming from inside the office probably weren't helping.

"Why are you quivering?" asked Maud. "Surely a scary witch like you can't be frightened of the Head?"

"I'm not f-f-frightened," said Penelope. "I'm just a little c-c-cold."

"It seems warm enough to me," said Maud, leaning back casually in her chair. She'd recently found out that the Head was actually the ghost of her great-aunt Ethel. So although she still found the Head a little spooky, she didn't think she'd punish them too severely. After all, Maud was her great-niece.

"Enter," said a voice from inside. The large wooden door creaked open. The strange yowling stopped and a dozen pairs of green eyes gazed out of the dim room. Penelope tiptoed in, but Maud strode right through the doorway and plonked herself down on one of the large leather armchairs in front of the desk.

The cats mewed and rubbed themselves against Maud's legs, which made Quentin burrow deeper into her pocket.

Maud looked down at him. "We won't be here long," she whispered.

"You don't know that," said Penelope. "And stop talking to that stupid scaredy-rat of yours. Maybe I should bring my black cat Nightshade into school one day. Then he'd really have something to be nervous about."

As the silence stretched out, Maud began to wonder if this wasn't going to be as easy as she'd thought. This was a school for monsters, after all, so who knew what kind of horrible punishments might be in store? Would an ordinary human girl even be able to survive them?

The Head appeared out of thin air, making Maud and Penelope jump. She was sitting on the edge of her desk and peering down at them through her large round glasses. "Well, well, well," she said. "I hear you girls have been fighting."

"Maud started it," Penelope burst out.

"That's not true," said Maud. "You were being spiteful to my friend Paprika. You really upset him."

"She said there was a bunny rabbit behind me," said Penelope. "And there wasn't."

"That was obviously a joke," said Maud. "There was no need to cast a spell on me."

"Well, some things are too serious to joke about," said Penelope. "Isn't that right, Miss?"

"That's quite enough," said the Head. "I had to listen to enough petty squabbling when I was alive. I don't intend to waste my afterlife doing the same. Now, as I'm sure you'll know, sports day is just around the corner. You won't win anything unless you put aside these silly disagreements, will you?"

"No, Miss," said Maud and Penelope together.

"I think you two need to learn the value of working together," said the Head. "And that's why I'm going to ask that you stay behind after school to help out the caretaker, Mr Quasimodo, in the greenhouse. Now, off you go."

As they made their way out of the office and

down the dusty corridor, Maud let out a long sigh of relief. Gardening sounded boring, but it was much better than the kind of monster torture she'd been expecting.

Penelope, however, was shaking even more than before.

"I just don't see what's so bad about watering plants," said Maud.

"Well," said Penelope, "you've obviously never been into Mr Quasimodo's greenhouse."

A cold wind howled over the playing fields as Mr Quasimodo led Maud and a reluctant Penelope to the large greenhouse at the back of the school.

"This way," said Mr Quasimodo, shambling along with his arms swinging in front of him. He had green skin, patchy black hair and a stubby nose. Mr Quasimodo walked so bent over that his nose almost touched his knees.

"Mr Quasimodo's an ogre. He's married to the school nurse," whispered Penelope.

Maud nodded. They followed him through the overgrown wilderness beyond the playing field as the sun set behind the school. Before they'd set out, Mr Quasimodo had given them white protective body suits, heavy boots, orange gloves and clear plastic visors. It should have made Maud feel more comfortable, but it only made her more nervous about what was inside the greenhouse.

They passed a sign that read:

**DANGER DO NOT ENTER**

"Are you sure we're supposed to be here?" asked Maud.

But Mr Quasimodo simply repeated, "This way," and kept lurching onwards.

Maud could see the huge glass structure of the greenhouse looming at the edge of the dense forest that surrounded the school grounds.

She spotted another sign nailed to a tree:

NO LIVING STUDENTS
BEYOND THIS POINT

Penelope gulped loudly.

Maud could feel Quentin rummaging in her pocket. It was just as well he couldn't read.

They passed a third warning sign:

SERIOUSLY, IF YOU ARE
STILL HERE LEAVE NOW

Behind it, the Rotwood greenhouse towered up against the darkening sky.

It was the largest greenhouse Maud had ever seen, with a rusty metal framework housing hundreds of panes of glass. It was difficult to see in through the steamy windows, but Maud thought that the mass of greenery inside seemed to move around. Her stomach squirmed, and she silently cursed herself for getting into trouble.

Mr Quasimodo handed Maud a rusty key. "Lock after," he said. "Or big trouble."

He turned and lolloped back to the school.

"After you," said Maud.

"No thanks," said Penelope. "Tutus first."

Maud sighed. "Fine," she said, and placed the key into the weather-beaten lock, giving it a sharp twist. As she shoved the door open, vapours of steam trailed out into the cold evening air.

The greenhouse was swelteringly hot inside. Maud could feel beads of sweat forming on her forehead as soon as she entered.

Inside the huge building were countless rows of wooden trellises covered in dense green vines, so overgrown that they stretched all the way from the floor to the ceiling in places. And Maud hadn't been imagining things – the plants were moving. All around her, the vines twisted and wriggled like giant green worms.

In thick clay pots between the rows bright red flowers sprouted. They had spiky petals that looked like overgrown Venus flytraps. Each plant was the size of a tree. Maud could hear a low droning noise, but the vegetation grew so thickly she couldn't see what was making it.

Something swooped towards them. "Get down!" shouted Maud. She and Penelope threw themselves to the ground as the creature buzzed over them. It was a gigantic insect – a fly as big as a eagle. Just as it was about to turn and swoop down on them again, one of the red flowers lurched forwards and snapped its jaws shut around it.

There was a horrendous squishing noise, and black goo splattered down to the floor.

Quentin squeaked with fear inside Maud's pocket. For once, Maud knew how he felt.

Taking a deep breath, she got up and picked her way through tangled foliage over to the cupboard at the side of the greenhouse. "I suppose we'd better get on with it," she said, handing a mop to Penelope.

"I don't see why *I* should," said Penelope. "It's *your* fault we're here; you should do all the work."

"I'll do my half," said Maud, as she set about mopping up the pools of black gloop from underneath the plants. She cast the occasional glance upward in case any of them were looking hungry. The liquid was so thick that it was impossible to wring the mop out into the bucket. Grumbling loudly, Penelope made a start on the other side of the aisle.

Maud ignored her and got on with her tasks. Mopping up the sticky liquid had been tough, but watering the plants was even harder. Every time Maud tried to approach one of them with her watering can, it turned around and snapped at her.

"All right, Mr Plant," she said to one of them. "I'm not a fly. I'm trying to help you."

"It can't understand you," said Penelope. "It's just a plant. Although it's probably still more intelligent than most of your friends, especially that puny little vampire."

"Paprika happens to be very clever," said

Maud. "He beat you on that Werewolf History test last week, didn't he?"

By the time Maud had finished, she was hot and bothered, and her white protective suit was black with grime. She hurried back to the cupboard to return her mop and watering can. Penelope did the same, even though she hadn't got through her half of the plants yet.

"Are you sure you've finished?" asked Maud.

"What was that?" asked Penelope. "I thought I heard something."

"Stop trying to change the subject," said Maud.

"Down there," said Penelope, pointing to a rustling clump of vines on the floor.

A black and yellow caterpillar the size of a Labrador crawled out. It stopped to look at them with its antennae wiggling in the air, and then shuffled rapidly towards them.

Maud and Penelope screamed at the top of their voices, and dashed towards the door as fast as they could, the caterpillar scuttling after them. Maud felt one of it antennae brush against the back of her leg, and ran faster.

Penelope dived outside and Maud followed, slamming the door behind her.

# Chapter Three

By the time Maud and Penelope had made it back to the school and changed out of their suits, the last bus was pulling out of the driveway. Maud tried running after it, but it was no use. It disappeared into the gloom of Rotwood forest, leaving just a cloud of black exhaust fumes behind.

*Drat!* thought Maud. Now she'd have to walk home through the woods. And who knew what kind of dangerous creatures lurked among those trees?

They heard a noise and turned around.

It was the Head, who'd materialised on the driveway beside her.

"The buses have already gone, Miss," said Maud. "How can we get home?"

"This looks like another chance for you two to show that you can work together," said the Head. "Penelope, you've got your broomstick here, haven't you?"

"Er … yes," said Penelope.

"Well, why don't you give Maud a lift home?"

It wasn't quite what Maud had been hoping for. And more importantly, if Penelope found out that Maud lived in an ordinary human house on an ordinary human street, she'd realise Maud wasn't a real monster, and she'd tell everyone.

"On second thoughts, I think I might walk," said Maud. "It's such a nice evening, after all."

Grey rainclouds swept across the school grounds from the dark forest.

"No, it isn't," said the Head, firmly. "Not even

a nocturnal ghoul could count this as a 'nice evening'. I'm sure Penelope will be happy to help."

"Actually, Miss," said Penelope. "My parents will be expecting me back soon so—"

"So all the more reason to get Maud home quickly," interrupted the Head.

Penelope trudged over to the broom shed and cast an unlocking spell on her broom. She carried it back over to Maud and climbed on.

"Well, what are you waiting for?" she asked.

Maud clambered on to the back of the broom and tried to make herself comfortable. Couldn't they at least put saddles on these things? And shouldn't she be wearing some sort of crash helmet?

Penelope glanced back at her. "You have ridden a broomstick before, haven't you?"

"Of course," said Maud, trying to lounge back casually and almost falling off.

"Good," said Penelope, "I'm in a hurry."

"Play nicely, girls," shouted the Head, as the stick shot up like a rocket.

Maud clung on desperately to Penelope's waist as the stick hurtled into the sky. A cold wind blew so hard into her face that at first she had to close her eyes. By the time she'd managed to open them again, she could see the whole of the school grounds stretching out beneath her, circled by the dark green forest.

Penelope's stick wobbled flimsily as she flew into the strong wind, and Maud had to shift back and forth to keep her balance.

They were now floating high in the air, swooping over the edge of the wood and passing the suburbs of the town, where the first streetlights of the evening were flickering on. Soon, Maud could see the spacious playing fields of her old school, Primrose Towers.

"Keep still," said Penelope. "If you're going to make me fly you home, the least you can do is stop fidgeting."

"I didn't make you fly me home," said Maud. "You're the one who got us into this mess."

"I wouldn't have tied Paprika's laces together if he'd been playing well," said Penelope.

"That's not true," said Maud. "He would have caught Mr Galahad's head if you'd left him alone."

Penelope turned round and jabbed Maud in the chest with one of her thin fingers. "He wouldn't have caught it in a million years!"

"Look out!" shouted Maud.

They were heading straight for a lamppost. The witch turned back just in time to swerve out of the way, but she couldn't keep the broom under control. The next moment they were plummeting to the ground. Maud closed her eyes and clung on to the stick.

The broom crashed into the ground with a jolt that sent Maud spinning through the air. Luckily, she landed in something soft.

Maud opened her eyes and saw she was lying in a privet hedge in the garden of a semi-detached house. A few feet away from her, the broom had planted itself into the garden with such force that it had ripped up a strip of turf. And Penelope was in a heap by the roses.

Maud looked into her pocket to check on Quentin. He was curled at the bottom of it and shaking with fright, but he didn't seem to be hurt. She decided she'd give him an extra helping of milk and crisps tonight to make up for his ordeal.

The door of the house swung open and the porch light came on. "Goodness, are you all right?" came a voice from inside.

Maud wondered why she recognised the voice. *Mum!* thought Maud. She'd landed in her own front garden.

Her mum was standing in the open doorway of their house and staring at Maud through her large round glasses. She was wearing her beige cardigan and green skirt, and holding a needle and thread.

"What's going on?" asked Maud's mum. "Why have you stuck a broom in the middle of the garden?"

"It's a scarecrow," said Maud. "I thought it might be useful to put one up."

"But we don't have any crows," said her mum.

"Well ... er ... this will keep it that way," said Maud.

Her mum looked over at Penelope, who was scrambling to her feet and dusting herself down. "Is this a friend from school?"

"Not exactl—" began Maud.

“Hello there,” said Maud’s mum. “I’m Mrs Montague. We were just about to eat dinner. Would you like to join us?”

Maud stared at Penelope, desperately hoping she would say ‘no’. The last thing she needed was for Penelope to find out that Maud had a normal human family.

Unfortunately, a nasty grin spread across Penelope’s face. “Yes, please, Mrs Montague,” she said. “That would be absolutely delightful.”

# Chapter Four

Milly smiled smugly.

"I got ten out of ten on my History test. I knew I would."

Maud, Penelope and Mr Montague were sitting around the dining table and listening to Maud's twin sister Milly chattering about her day at Primrose Towers.

Maud never bothered trying to tell her parents anything about her own school day. Whenever she did, Milly would interrupt her and keep going until she'd described every last detail of hers. Not that Maud minded. She was trying to keep it a secret from her parents that Rotwood was a school for monsters, so the less she said about it the better.

"Then Farmer Gilbert from Buttercup Farm came in to visit us," continued Milly. "And he brought a little baby lamb with him, and we all got to feed it with a bottle of milk. It was so cute. I took loads of photos."

*Well, at least Penelope has to listen to this too*, Maud thought. It was probably a worse punishment than anything the Head could have thought up.

"And on Friday we've got sports day and the pupil who Mrs Fennel thinks has done best will win a ride to Buttercup Farm on a Shetland pony called Prancer and they'll get to feed all the little calves and foals and piglets. Can you imagine how tiny and precious they'll be?"

Maud glanced across at Penelope and was pleased to see that she'd gone pale from Milly's description of the cute farmyard animals. With any luck, Penelope would soon run screaming for the door.

When Milly finally ran out of things to say, Maud's dad turned to Penelope. "So, Penelope, how long have you been at Rotwood, then?"

"Since the start of Year 1," she said. "Most of us have. That's why we were so surprised when Maud joined last week."

"She was transferred from her old school," said Mr Montague. "Didn't she tell you?"

"And which school was that?" asked Penelope, glancing suspiciously at Maud. Maud felt her cheeks going red. If only her dad would keep quiet ...

"Primrose Towers School for Girls," said Mr Montague. "The school that Milly goes to."

"I'm very popular there," said Milly. "That's why they didn't expel me. Everyone used to call Maud 'Monstrous'."

"She's not that monstrous, if you ask me," said Penelope.

"She's not at all monstrous!" said Mr Montague loyally, not realising that at Rotwood, being 'monstrous' was a good thing. "And Milly, remember we prefer to say that Maud was *transferred*, not expelled. To somewhere she would fit better. Like that time I took the rubber car mats out of my brother's Honda saloon and put them in my Volvo estate."

"Primrose Towers?" asked Penelope. "That's pretty strange, if you ask me. I mean, strange for a mons—"

"Food's here!" shouted Maud. She'd spotted her mum walking in with a huge pot of spaghetti Bolognese, and she didn't like the way the conversation was going.

"That's a splendid costume," said Mrs Montague, looking at Penelope's ragged black dress and large pointy hat. "Are you doing the *Wizard of Oz* at school?"

"Are we doing what to the *Wizard of Oz*?" asked Penelope. "I have a cousin who's a wizard, but he lives in Manchester, not Oz."

"Er … no," said Mrs Montague, smiling. "I make costumes for the local amateur dramatics society, you see. I've always wanted to do something like that, with pointy hats and fake warts. Can I touch that one on the end of your nose? I'd love to see what it's made of."

Maud coughed loudly and leaped up between the two of them. "Her warts are real!" she whispered. "Don't mention them."

"Oops," said Mrs Montague. "Sorry, dear."

"So," said Mr Montague, "tell us, Penelope, wart lessons … I mean, *what* lessons do you enjoy at school?"

"Same as everyone else," said Penelope. "Fright Classes."

"Beg your pardon?" asked Mr Montague.

"She means 'Write Classes'," said Maud. "That's what we call English lessons at Rotwood. This is fun, isn't it? Anyway, I'll serve the spaghetti." Maud picked up the spoon and dipped it into the wide metal pot.

"That's nice, dear," said Mrs Montague, sounding a little surprised but pleased that Maud had volunteered so readily.

"I can do it instead if you like," said Milly. "Maud will probably get it wrong."

"No, that's all right," said Mrs Montague. "Give her a chance."

Maud picked up a bowl and was just about to spoon out some of the pasta when she noticed that the food was moving around. It wasn't spaghetti at all – it was worms! Maud looked over at Penelope, who gave her a knowing smile. She'd clearly been casting spells again. And worst of all, it looked like she'd figured out Maud's secret.

Maud slammed down the lid on the squirming pot. "Do you know, I think it needs more salt," she said and hurried it back into the kitchen.

"I'm sure it's fine," said Mr Montague. "Too

much salt is bad for you, anyway. Like putting petrol in a diesel car."

*Not as bad for you as too many worms,* thought Maud, emptying the pot into the bin. When she was finished, she stopped to think for a moment, and then threw the pot on to the floor with a huge clang.

"Whoops!" shouted Maud. "I've dropped it!"

"I told you she'd get it wrong," yelled Milly triumphantly. "You should have let me do it."

Maud popped her head around the kitchen door. "Oh well," she said, "it's too late now. Why don't we get a Chinese takeaway instead? I'll find the menu."

"Well, I suppose we'll have to," said Mr Montague. "That's a shame. I was looking forward to that."

"Never mind," said Mrs Montague. "I'm sure Maud couldn't help it."

"Sorry, Mum," said Maud. She cast a glance at Penelope. "But on the bright side, it'll give us time to look at Milly's photos of that cute little lamb."

"What a good idea!" said Mrs Montague.

Milly's eyes lit up. "Just wait until you see him," she said, fishing around in her bag for her camera phone. "He was such a scrummy little lambikins."

"Actually, I'm not that hungry," said Penelope, who looked as if she'd swallowed sour milk. "It's getting late, so I'd better go."

Penelope hurried out of the door into the front garden. Through the window, Maud noticed her pull her broomstick out of the earth. Maud dashed over and pulled the curtains shut before her family could see their guest float away on a cleaning tool.

As she sat down again, she felt her heart slow down to a normal pace. Thank goodness Penelope had gone, but she wished her parents hadn't told her about Primrose Towers. Now her worst enemy would know for sure that

Maud was a normal girl. And you could bet your eyeballs that Penelope would find a way to use it against her.

# Chapter Five

The next morning, Maud followed the other pupils from her class off the school bus as usual. She was just about to make her way over to the main entrance when she stopped in her tracks.

Writhing green vines completely covered the front of the school. The plants were snaking across Rotwood's grey stones, wrapping themselves around the leering gargoyles and blocking out the windowpanes.

Mr Quasimodo was up his ladder, trying to chop the tangled vines down from the front of the building with a huge pair of shears. He stopped to glower at Maud as she approached.

A shiver ran through her. These were the same plants she'd seen in the greenhouse last night! How had they got all the way to the school …?

"No!" gasped Maud, slapping her forehead as she remembered Mr Quasimodo's words:

*Lock after, or big trouble.*

Wilf ran around the corner, howling with excitement. "Come and see this," he shouted, waving everyone round to the back of the school. They all ran after him, and Maud followed, dread gathering in the pit of her stomach.

She heard loud gasps as she turned the corner. The entire playing field was covered with gigantic Venus flytraps, just like the ones Maud had been watering the previous night.

Now the plants had escaped from their pots, they'd grown into a seething mass, with thick green stems twisting and jerking, tough roots churning up the soil and red flowers chomping angrily at the air. Every time a bird flew overhead, the flowers would snap up at it one by one.

"Most regrettable," came a voice from behind Maud. She turned around to see her teacher Mr Von Bat shaking his head. "It looks like someone forgot to lock the greenhouse door …" He raised an eyebrow at Maud, and she cringed with shame.

"You'd all better get inside," said Mr Von Bat. "The Head has called a special assembly to discuss this little … incident."

Maud trudged inside with the rest of the pupils, desperately hoping the Head wouldn't make an example of her in front of everyone.

Rotwood's main hall was a cavernous vault with an arched ceiling and lines of crumbling stone pillars. Narrow windows set high in the wall threw shafts of light through the dusty air on to the cobweb-covered walls.

The pupils took their places on rows of hard wooden pews that faced a pipe organ and an ancient wooden lectern bearing the Rotwood crest and the school motto:

**BECAUSE WE SCARE**

A nervous murmur broke out as the ghostly form of the Head floated in through the back wall and stood behind the lectern. Even the vampires, witches and werewolves of Rotwood seemed to find the Head a little spooky.

"I'm afraid I've got bad news for you all," said the Head. "As you will have noticed, the school has a severe vegetation problem. The playing field is now covered with greenery so dense and vicious that it will take poor Mr Quasimodo at least a fortnight to prune it all back. As a result, I'm afraid we're going to have to cancel this year's sports day."

Cries and groans echoed around the hall. Wilf and his older brother Warren let out mournful howls. Maud knew they'd both had their hearts set on winning medals this year.

A few rows ahead, Maud saw Penelope stick up her hand.

"Be quiet now," said the Head. "Penelope has something to say."

Maud could guess what she was up to. Penelope was going to pin the whole disaster on her and claim she'd had nothing to do with it.

The other monsters quietened down as Penelope stood up. "I know how we can still have sports day," she said.

That wasn't quite what Maud had expected. The Head peered at Penelope over the top of her round glasses. "And how might that be?"

"We could use the Primrose Towers playing field. I flew over it last night and it's absolutely massive. Plus, Maud Montague's sister Milly goes there, so Maud can get her parents to ask the head teacher at Primrose Towers."

Maud shrank down in her pew as Penelope turned round to look at her with a smug grin on her face. All the other pupils stared at Maud too, and she could hear them muttering things like, "That's funny, I thought Primrose Towers was a human school?" and "Why would any decent monster go to a horrible place like that?"

"I'm not so sure," said the Head. "We'd have to be very careful. Humans and monsters don't always mix well, you know."

She glanced at Maud, and Maud could have sworn she winked.

"However," said the Head, "I don't see the harm in asking. Especially if we can have the whole field to ourselves. What do you think, Miss Montague?"

Maud didn't know what to say. She didn't like the idea of letting the Rotwood monsters and the prim Primrose Towers girls get too close to each other. But on the other hand, she felt very guilty about leaving the greenhouse door open. The whole situation was partly her fault, so she really ought to help. And if nothing else, it might prevent her being given a further punishment by the Head.

"All right," said Maud. "I'll ask my mum about it."

The Rotwood monsters all broke into applause. "Yesssss!" called out Wilf. "You're totally monstrous, Maud!"

But as Maud looked around, she saw one monster who wasn't cheering. Paprika was sitting at the end of a row, with his head in his hands. Of course! He'd obviously have preferred it if sports day hadn't happened at all, so he wouldn't have to play more Monsterball. And now Maud felt guilty all over again.

*Everything I do seems to to upset somebody these days,* thought Maud, sadly.

# Chapter Six

After dinner that evening, Maud sat on the stairs under the long diagonal row of Montague family portraits. Quentin stuck his front legs over the hem of her pocket and looked up at her with his tiny black eyes.

Maud stroked his head and sighed. "What do you think, Quentin? Maybe I should just pretend we asked Primrose Towers if we could use their playing field, and that they said no."

Quentin looked up at the portrait of Maud's great-aunt Ethel that was hanging above them and trembled.

"I suppose you're right," said Maud. "I promised I'd ask, so I've got to do it."

Maud got up and went down to the living room, where her mum was reading a book about costume design called *Theatrical Threads*.

"Mum, could you do me a favour?" asked Maud.

"What is it, dear?" asked Mrs Montague.

"Could you ring Mrs Fennel at Primrose Towers and ask if we can use their playing field for our sports day?"

"Why can't you hold it at your school?" asked Mrs Montague.

"We've got some, er … weeds growing on our field," said Maud.

Milly barged in. Maud might have known she couldn't mention Primrose Towers without her twin sister's ears pricking up.

"You can't use our playing field!" she shouted. "We've got our own sports day this week. It's on Saturday. I've been chosen for the backwards running race, because it's the most difficult event of all."

"We could have ours on Friday," said Maud. "That way everyone would get to have a sports day."

"That sounds fair," said Mrs Montague. "I'll ask Mrs Fennel what she thinks."

Milly glared at Maud as their mum walked out of the room to get her phone.

"You just want to bring your weird Rotwood friends to my school, don't you?" said Milly. "So they can mess everything up."

"No," said Maud. In fact, she'd much rather be keeping the Rotwood monsters and Primrose Towers girls apart, for both their sakes.

Mrs Montague came back into the room. "That's settled then," she said. "Mrs Fennel says that the Rotwood students are welcome to use the playing fields on Friday, and Primrose Towers can go ahead with their sports day on Saturday."

“Thanks,” said Maud, while Milly groaned and rolled her eyes. Maud knew how she felt. It wasn’t as if she wanted their sports day to be held at Primrose Towers either.

Afterwards, Maud took Quentin back to his cage in the garage for an evening treat of milk and crisps.

“I wish I was as carefree as you,” she said, filling his bowl.

Just as she said this, Quentin heard the distant meow of a cat and scuttled to the back of his cage, curling into a ball.

“Well, maybe a little *more* carefree than you,” said Maud. “But at least you don’t have to pretend to be a scary monster called a Tutu all the time, when you’re really just an ordinary girl. And at least you don’t end up upsetting everyone when you try to help them.”

Maud thought about how miserable Paprika had looked when he realised sports day was back on. She was going to have to do something about that, and fast. Sports day was on Friday, and today was Tuesday. That meant she had two days to turn Paprika into a decent sportsman.

Well, she had to try at least.

# Chapter Seven

The next day 3B and 2C had Monsterball practice again. They were having extra PE lessons every afternoon until sports day, so Fright Classes were cancelled for the week.

The playing field was still out of bounds because of the plant infestation. Mr Quasimodo had tried attacking the plants with his lawnmower, but they'd eaten it and he'd had to flee for his own safety.

So, instead, they were practising in the main hall. They pushed the pews to the side, but it still didn't make much of a pitch.

It was just too cramped and dim, with the only light coming from the high windows and the flickering candelabras at the front of the hall.

Even so, Maud managed to enjoy it. She was really getting the hang of Monsterball now, and found herself weaving in and out of Class 2C's defenders with ease, as Quentin clung on to her shoulder. Penelope hadn't bothered her all game, which she thought was a little odd. At one point Maud was sure she'd even smiled at her. She must have been imagining it.

Odder still was the fact that Penelope hadn't picked on Paprika once, even though he missed Mr Galahad's head every single time it was passed to him. He had even run into his own teammates twice. If Maud was honest, she'd have to say that the team would be better off without him playing at all.

At one point, Wilf passed to Paprika when he was just a couple of metres away from the goal. For once, Paprika managed to catch the head. Maud couldn't believe it – he was certain to score from there! But Paprika launched the helmeted head in the wrong direction, and it crashed into a candlestick at the front of the hall. It toppled over, splattering wax everywhere.

"Never mind, let's move on to Stag-beetle-jousting instead," said Mr Galahad.

Maud had always rather liked beetles. She'd even tried to keep one as a pet in a jar under her bed until Milly had told their mum, and she'd been forced to throw it away. But she'd never heard of beetle *jousting*.

Mr Galahad led them out to the east side of the school, past Mr Quasimodo. The caretaker was on the highest rung of his ladder, furiously chopping down thorny vines into a huge pile below.

"I'm really sorry about all the extra work, Mr Quasimodo!" Maud called up.

The caretaker glared at her and went on with his pruning.

Fifty metres along a forest track, partly hidden from the school, five slimy-looking cave mouths gaped from a rock face. Maud had never been to this part of the forest before. Mr Galahad went up to the first cave and whistled. Maud could hear the sound of shuffling legs echoing around the deep cave, until eventually a large pair of horns emerged from the shadows. A moment later, a beetle the size of a pony lumbered out.

Maud blinked and rubbed her eyes, but when she lowered her hands, the enormous beetle was still there. Quentin leapt straight into her pocket, leaving just his pink tail sticking out of the top. Maud felt like running away too, but she didn't want anyone to see she was frightened.

"Right, Montague," said Mr Galahad. "You can ride Perky. He's in the third cave along. Off you trot!"

Maud had no choice but to approach the dark entrance. She tiptoed closer, and began to make out a huge shadowy form inside the cave.

"Here, boy," she said, telling herself that the beetle was just a pet like any other. He trundled out and brushed his antlers against her. They felt hard and slippery, like her gran's polished mahogany dining table. Maud forced herself to smile and pet the antlers. "That's right," she said. "There's a good boy."

Perky crouched down to let Maud on. Even when he was stooping towards her, the beetle came up to her chest, and it took her a couple of attempts to scramble on to his hard back.

When Maud had finally mounted the creature, she picked up the reins that were tied around his neck and squeezed his flanks with her legs. He lurched forward so jerkily that Maud thought she might slip off, but she managed to keep her balance and steer him round to the front of the school, where the rest of the class were lining up in two rows facing each other.

Next to her, Paprika was struggling to keep his beetle under control.

"What are the rules?" asked Maud.

"Same as any other beetle joust," said Paprika. "You just ride your beetle towards the opposite person and knock them off with its antlers."

"Sounds fun," said Maud, uncertainly.

"Not really," shrugged Paprika. "It's not as much fun as Monsterball."

"Why's that?"

"I'm not as good at this."

"Uh-oh," said Maud. "I mean, never mind. I'm sure you'll be all right."

Maud looked across at the opposite row. Her

opponent was Oscar, a boy from her class who wore a ruff, doublet and hose. Like Mr Galahad, he had a detachable head – but he was using both hands to hold on to the reins, so he'd had to leave it on the ground. Maud reckoned she had a fairly good chance against an opponent who couldn't see where he was going. Unfortunately, Paprika was opposite Wilf's gigantic werewolf brother Warren, so his chances of winning were pretty much zero.

Mr Galahad blew the whistle, and the jousting began.

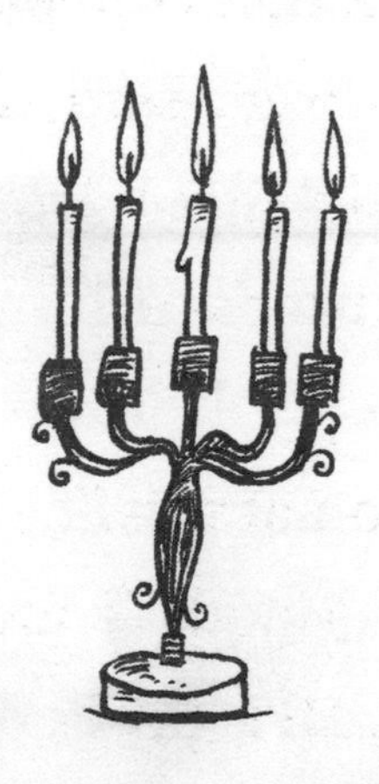

# Chapter Eight

Maud squeezed Perky's flanks and felt the beetle jolt beneath her as he charged ahead. She glanced back to see how Paprika was doing. He'd already managed to fall off his beetle before getting anywhere near Warren, and he was now flailing around on the floor while his beetle prodded him with its antlers. It looked as if the beetle just wanted to play, but even so, it was in danger of crushing the poor vampire.

Maud pulled hard on Perky's rein, forcing him to turn back in the opposite direction.

There were angry shouts as she weaved in and out of the other jousters, desperate to get to Paprika and save him from his peckish beetle.

"Shoo," Maud shouted. "Bad beetle!"

"Careful!" shouted Mr Galahad. "He doesn't understand you, Montague."

But Paprika's beetle looked up at Maud's words, tilting its head to one side as if it was listening.

"There, there, Mr Beetle," said Maud. She came up alongside and stroked its horns. "I don't think poor Paprika wants to play with you. So run along now."

The beetle moved its head up and down as if it was nodding, and then, without warning, set off at a run. Paprika was still clinging on to the reins, and the beetle dragged him across the ground for several metres before he thought to let go.

"That's not what I meant," called Maud, but it was too late. Paprika's beetle panicked all the other ones as it went, and they careered off in different directions.

One of the beetles ran right up against the side of the school, brushing past the ladder propped up there. It wobbled back and forth for a couple of seconds before crashing down to the ground. Mr Quasimodo plunged into a pile of thorny cuttings.

The caretaker got up and waved his shears in the air. His gaze fell on Maud and he growled ferociously.

"Yes, well, I think that's quite enough jousting for today," said Mr Galahad. "I suppose we'd better evacuate the area until Mr Quasimodo has had time to clear it. Let's make our way over to the obstacle course in an orderly fashion."

Wilf howled with delight.

"Is the obstacle course a bit easier?" asked Maud.

"No," said Wilf. "It's the hardest event of all. But I love it. It's totally monstrous. After all, sports day is all about challenging yourself, isn't it?"

"I suppose so," said Maud, though she wasn't convinced.

Mr Galahad rounded up all the stag beetles and herded them back into their caves. Perky seemed reluctant to leave Maud. "Don't worry," Maud told the beetle. "I'll come and visit you again." Perky rubbed his horns against her side before lumbering back to his cave.

When all the beetles were safely put away, Mr Galahad led the class deeper into the forest beyond. Above Maud, long branches entwined so tightly that she could barely see the sky. Thick black leaves crunched underfoot as they made their way down the path towards the course.

Soon they saw a sign:

**OBSTACLE COURSE**
**ENTER AT YOUR OWN RISK**

"Are you sure this is safe?" asked Maud.

"Of course, young'un," said Mr Galahad. "We only lost two students last year, a school record, no less!"

There was only space for six pupils to compete at a time and Maud was placed in the second group with Wilf. Paprika was in the first group, and Maud watched as they raced off into the murky forest. Soon they were out of sight, but she could hear screams coming from their direction. Maud hoped they were screams of excitement.

Mr Galahad blew his whistle and Maud's group set off. At first the course seemed to be nothing more than a straight path through the woods, and she couldn't understand what all the fuss was about. Then her foot hit something and she tripped, tumbling to the ground. As she scrambled back to her feet, hundreds of tiny money spiders showered down into her hair. *Well*, she thought, stopping to pick them out one by one. *At least they'll bring me good luck.*

Wilf ran past, shouting, "I can't believe you fell for the old spider trap. Don't you know anything?"

Maud looked back at the course and saw that she'd actually fallen over a tripwire that had been attached to a net in the tree above. She'd have to be more careful from now on.

A few moments later, she was racing towards a pile of leaves that had been swept into the middle of the path. But as she got closer, a gust of wind blew through the leaves, and Maud caught a glimpse of the wood of a trapdoor below them. Heart pounding, she jumped over the pile, trying not to think about what might be underneath it.

Maud was exhausted now, but the course wasn't over yet. She turned a corner to find a narrow plank over a pond of bubbling green goo that smelled of rotten fish. She edged along the plank, concentrating on her steps rather than on the repulsive stench. Even when she saw a sticky purple tentacle emerge from the pond, she just ignored it and kept going until she was safely across.

After that, Maud had to climb up a wall covered in black slime and crash down into a muddy ditch on the other side. She was exhausted, and she'd finished last in her group. But at least she hadn't lost a limb – or worse.

Maud stood up and scanned for Paprika to check he was all right. Everyone else from his group was sitting on the ground and getting their breath back, but he was nowhere to be seen.

Just then, Maud heard a loud splash and a familiar cry. She ran back, past the wall and all the way to the pond, where she saw that Paprika had tripped over his cape and fallen into the swirling goo.

As she raced up to him, Paprika dragged himself out of the stinky pond. He looked pretty shaken.

"Are you okay?" asked Maud.

"I'm fine," said Paprika. "Totally monstrous." Though he didn't sound it.

Maud could hear the gloop squelching inside Paprika's shoes as they walked back to the rest of the class, around the wall and the ditch. A few pupils sniggered when they saw him, but most of them looked concerned. Maud kept expecting Penelope to shout out something spiteful, but when she looked around, she noticed the witch wasn't even there. Maybe she was still completing the course. But when the last few pupils plopped over the top of the slime wall, she wasn't with them.

What was Penelope playing at?

# Chapter Nine

Maud tried not to breathe in.

"I wouldn't worry about it," she said. Maud was sitting on a mossy grave in the playground with Paprika, who still stank, but was trying to dry out his cape in the sun. "It doesn't matter if you aren't the best at sports. There are other things you're good at."

She tried to think of some examples. He was *quite* good at changing into a bat, but then, all vampires could do that. It would be a bit like telling a human they were good at breathing.

"Are you worried about your dad?" asked

Maud. "Do you think he'll be cross if you don't do well on sports day?"

"No, he wouldn't particularly care," said Paprika. "It's Mum I'm worried about."

That made sense. At the end of her first week of Rotwood, Maud had discovered that Paprika's dad, Mr Von Bat, wasn't a real vampire. He was just a human who was pretending to be one so he could keep teaching at the monster school. But Paprika's mum was a genuine vampire, and Maud guessed she could be pretty fearsome.

"I'm sure your mum will be pleased as long as you try your best," said Maud.

"No, she won't," he said. "She always says that trying your best isn't good enough. It's like when I was learning to fly. I tried and tried, but I just couldn't do it. In the end, she lost patience and threw me out of the upstairs window. Luckily I landed in a bush."

"Surely she wouldn't take sports day so seriously," said Maud.

"Yes, she will," said Paprika. "She'll go ballistic if I don't win a medal. 'Fangs come first', that's what she always says. She thinks witches and werewolves are inferior, so I'll be in trouble if I get beaten by Penelope or Warren."

No wonder Paprika was so worried about sports day. Maud was starting to feel guilty about saving it again.

"I know!" she said. "I'll help you train for a medal. And I'll get Wilf involved too. He loves sports and he's completely monstrous at most of them, so I bet he'll show you how to win."

"Really?" said Paprika.

"Really," said Maud.

Paprika smiled at last.

On her way back to class, Quentin stuck his nose out of Maud's pocket and sniffed.

"What is it?" she asked.

The rat slipped out of her blazer, scampered down her skirt, and leapt on to the floor. He threw a quick glance back at Maud and scurried down the corridor.

*Where's he going?* Maud wondered, running after him. Quentin paused at a corner and peeped around. Maud did the same, and spotted Penelope sneaking down the passage to the Head's office. That was weird. Penelope was scared of the Head, so what was she doing heading that way? Quentin had a good nose for trouble, so Maud decided to follow the witch and find out.

She gathered her pet back into her pocket and crept after Penelope.

The witch knocked on the door of the Head's office, listened for a few moments and then went inside. Maud followed Penelope, tiptoeing up to the door and putting her ear to it.

She couldn't hear much above the din of the

cats, but at one point she thought she heard the Head saying, "A swap, that's right. Perfect."

Then Maud heard the phone being slammed down, and footsteps coming over to the door. She tried to sneak back down the corridor, but the door swung open, and Penelope spotted her.

"What are you doing here?" asked Penelope, her eyes narrowing as she closed the door.

"I was just popping in to see the Head," said Maud.

"Well, there's no point," said Penelope. "I just saw her do her ghostly vanishing thing, so she isn't there any more."

"Never mind," said Maud. "What were you seeing her about, by the way?"

"Um … the Head just wanted a word with me," said Penelope. "It's not important."

"What was she saying about a swap?" asked Maud.

"I was asking if I could swap from Elementary Cauldron-stirring Class and try Advanced

Broomstick Tutorial instead," said Penelope. "Not that it's any of your business."

Penelope stormed off down the corridor. *Sometimes*, Maud thought, *I don't understand that witch at all. I thought she was supposed to be terrified of the Head.*

"Let's do this!" said Wilf.

It was break time the following morning, and Maud and Wilf were dashing down the spiral stairs to the playground with Paprika to fit in a quick training session.

"I'm sure Paprika just hasn't found the right sport yet," said Wilf, bouncing down the last few steps. "We'll fix that."

The Rotwood playground was a vast graveyard that stretched out to the west of the school. Most of the pupils were milling around the graves nearest to the building, so Wilf led them out to a quiet area at the back.

"Let's have a go at grave-hurdling," said Wilf. "You'll love this, Paprika. Try and jump over those ten graves in less than a minute. Come on, you can do it!"

Paprika got into position in front of the first grave and focused on it for a second. Then he darted forward and pushed off as hard as he could, clearing it with ease. Maud and Wilf cheered, and Paprika grinned at them. Unfortunately, he was so busy grinning that he smacked right into the second gravestone. He bounced off and fell with a thump on to the mossy ground.

"Never mind," said Maud. "Keep going."

Paprika picked himself up and ran towards the next stone. He managed to clamber over it, but he fell down the other side and landed awkwardly on his foot with a yelp. He scrambled up and limped onwards.

Maud was about to suggest he took things a bit slower, when the ground suddenly erupted nearby. Soil fell away from an open coffin lid and a skeleton popped its head out. "What's all this racket?" it asked. "Some of us are trying to sleep!"

"Sorry," said Maud. She wondered if the skeleton worked nights, like Mr Porter across the street from her house.

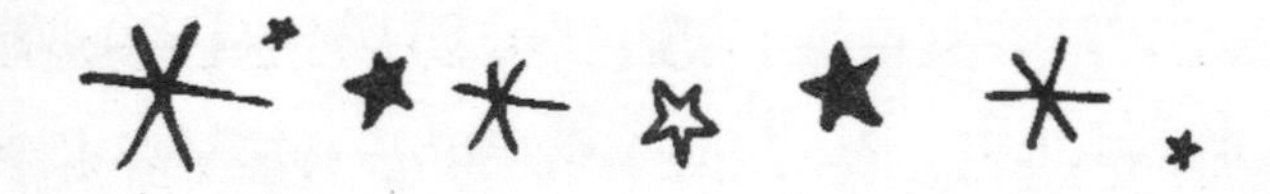

Time was running out, so at lunch break they decided to practise instead of going to the canteen. Wilf took them to a swamp near the edge of the forest. The dark green pool stretched away into the distance, flanked on all sides by gnarly roots and clumps of rotting leaves.

"Have a go at swamp-swimming," Wilf said. "You've never tried that. It might be your thing."

He glanced at Maud and shrugged doubtfully. "Okay," said Paprika. "What do I have to do?"

"Just jump in and swim to the end and back," said Wilf. "I'll show you."

Wilf took off his jacket and plunged into the swamp. He showed Paprika the 'beast stroke', pushing his paws out to the side, bobbing his head up and down and howling. This swamp wasn't quite as stinky as the one in the obstacle course, but Maud still didn't fancy sticking her head into it. She couldn't stand the thought of that slime getting into her eyes and ears. Plus, there were a few bubbles rising to the surface, and Maud couldn't help wondering if something was lurking under there.

Paprika handed Maud his cape and sploshed in. He flailed his arms around in the gloopy liquid for a few seconds before sinking beneath the surface.

"Wilf!" shouted Maud. "I think Paprika's drowning!"

Maud pointed to the spot where Paprika had been and Wilf held his nose and dived down. A few seconds later, he emerged with one of his paws around Paprika's chest.

"Are you all right?" asked Maud.

Paprika coughed out a mouthful of gloop in reply.

Wilf pulled Paprika into the shallows, waded out of the swamp, shook his fur dry and tried to pull the half-vampire out. Maud grabbed Paprika's arm and tried to pull too, but it was no use. He was stuck fast. Maud looked down at his leg and saw that there was a scaly green hand clamped around it.

"1 … 2 … 3," said Wilf, and they both pulled at once. This time the slimy green claw lost its grip, and they pulled Paprika to the shore.

As soon as the vampire was back on dry land, they propped him up and guided him back towards the school.

Behind them, the swamp creature Paprika

had disturbed was standing in the shallows of the pool with its hands on its hips. It had green gills, huge fishy lips and glassy black eyes. "If you're going to drop snacks on my doorstep," it said, "you could at least let me finish them."

The sun had broken through the grey clouds as they reached the edge of the grass, so they sat down for a moment to dry out.

"Why didn't you tell us you couldn't swim?" asked Maud.

"I didn't want to disappoint you," said Paprika.

"We'd have been a bit more than disappointed if you'd been eaten by that swamp monster," said Maud.

"It doesn't matter," sniffed Paprika. "I think Mum would prefer me to be eaten by a Swamp Thing than to come away from sports day without a medal."

"That can't be true," said Maud.

"Yes, it is," said Paprika. "I'm not going to

win anything and she's going to ground me for ever."

Maud wondered if Paprika's mum would really be so hard on her own son. She'd never met any other vampires, so she couldn't really judge. But she'd heard they could be a rotten bunch.

"I'm sure you'll win something," said Maud. But the truth was, even she didn't believe it any more. Sports day was tomorrow, and they still hadn't managed to find something Paprika was good at.

Maud woke up the next morning feeling very confused. In her dream, she'd been chosen to compete in a flying race as part of sports day. Not only could she fly, she was flying brilliantly, swooping up and down in the air with ease. Then, just as she was about to cross the finish line, she found herself plummeting to the ground. Seconds before she crashed into it, she jerked awake.

"Drat!" she said, looking at her clock. She had overslept by half an hour. It was hardly surprising, given the amount of training she'd been doing, but it meant she was going to have to rush if she wanted to catch the school bus and be ready for sports day.

Maud flung her clothes on, brushed her teeth, grabbed her games kit and raced downstairs. As she was leaving, she noticed that her parents were getting ready to go out too. Mrs Montague was packing sandwiches into a plastic container, while Mr Montague was filling up his travel flask with coffee.

"You're not coming to my sports day, are you?" asked Maud.

"Why?" asked Mrs Montague. "Are we really such an embarrassment?"

They were pretty embarrassing, in fact. When Maud had gone to Primrose Towers, her dad had turned every conversation at parents' evening round to the topic of cars, and her mum had clapped so loudly every time she was on stage in the school play that nobody could hear anything she said. But that wasn't the problem.

The last thing Maud wanted was for her parents to realise she went to a school for monsters, and force her to leave.

"No," said Maud, "not at all. I just don't think it will be very interesting for you."

Maud's mum continued packing her lunch. Maud thought this was odd, but she didn't have time to question it. They were probably off to another of her dad's vintage car shows.

On her way out, Maud popped into the garage to say goodbye to Quentin.

"I'm going to leave you at home today," she said as she filled up his crisp bowl. "I don't think all that loud cheering would be good for you."

The bus was pulling away from the stop as Maud arrived, so she ran alongside it, waving frantically at everyone to get the driver to stop and let her in. The bus pulled up a few feet down the road.

"If you run as well as that today you're bound to win a medal," said Mr Galahad, who was sitting in one of the front seats, his head resting on his knee. It seemed even the teachers were riding on the buses for sports day.

Maud made her way down the bus to the empty seat next to Paprika. The pupils were wearing bulky hats, scarves and coats to disguise their appearances, just as they always did when they were outside Rotwood.

Paprika turned to Maud as she sat down next to him. He looked pale, even by the usual standards of vampires, so she smiled to reassure him. Paprika tried to smile back, but it looked more as if he was about to cry.

The bus chugged off down the road. Except today, instead of turning left into the forest like usual, it drove straight on. As it went, it was joined by other Rotwood buses from different parts of town, until at last they all reached Primrose Towers.

It was weird, Maud thought, seeing her old school again. She'd become so used to the crumbling stone and leering gargoyles of Rotwood that the clean red brick and spotless windows of Primrose Towers seemed even cleaner and more spotless than they had before.

Several of the Rotwood pupils let out cries of horror when they saw the Primrose Towers girls in the playground dressed in their neat navy uniforms.

"Gross," said Oscar. "That girl's got pigtails. Is she wearing fancy dress or something?"

"Urgh!" cried a voice next to him that must have been Invisible Isabel. "Those girls have got teddy-bear backpacks on. Why don't their teachers stop them?"

"What's wrong with the building?" asked Wilf. "There's hardly any grime on it and none of the windows are broken."

"That's such a strange playground," said Oscar. "Where are the gravestones, and the mausoleums and the crypts?"

"These humans are a bit odd, if you ask me," said Isabel. Maud was glad that the Primrose Towers playing field was a good distance from the school. She really didn't want the Rotwood pupils to bump into her old schoolmates.

"Are you all right?" she asked Paprika, who was sitting in silence next to her.

"Sort of," he said. "Can you help me put this on? Mum said it will protect my skin. Vampires aren't great with sunshine, you know."

Paprika handed Maud a tube of Factor 500 sunscreen and she rubbed it into his neck. As if he didn't have enough to worry about without the sun burning him.

Maud's bus spluttered to a halt on the immaculate grass of the Primrose Towers playing fields, and the other buses pulled up alongside. The Rotwood pupils stepped outside and began to peel off their bulky jackets, hats and scarves.

Just as they were starting to unload their equipment from the battered trunk of the bus, Maud looked back at the school and saw something that made her gasp. A vast crowd of Primrose Towers pupils, along with Mrs Fennel, was heading towards them. And even worse, they were all dressed in white sports kit.

"Human alert!" shouted Maud, and the Rotwood pupils raced back on to the buses to put their disguises on again.

"What are they doing here?" asked Wilf.

"Quiet everyone," said Mr Von Bat. Then he turned to Mr Galahad. "We'd better go and sort this out," he said. "But first, you really ought to put your head back on."

Mr Galahad had been bouncing his head on the ground while he was waiting for the pupils to unload the equipment from the van. "Oh dear," he said, and plonked it back on his shoulders. It was definitely an improvement, but he was still going to look a little strange to the Primrose Towers girls with his full suit of armour. And Mr Von Bat was hardly going to blend in with his black cape, pointed fangs and slicked-back hair.

"You two are coming as well," said Mr Von Bat to Maud and Penelope. "After all, it was your idea to come here."

Maud wanted to point out that it had been Penelope's idea and not hers, but it didn't seem the right time. The Primrose Towers girls were approaching, so they hurried over to meet them.

Maud noticed a few of the girls pointing at her and muttering to each other: "That's Monstrous Maud," and, "You know, the one who was expelled," but she did her best to ignore them. Anyway, she wasn't the only one getting funny looks. Mrs Fennel was examining Mr Von Bat as if he was a slug she'd just found in her salad.

"There must be some misunderstanding," said Mrs Fennel. "Today is Friday."

"Indeed it is," said Mr Galahad. "And Friday is the day we're holding our sports day on your fields. We're having ours today and you're having yours tomorrow. I believe it was Maud Montague's mother who made the arrangement with you."

There was a tide of whispering among the Primrose Towers girls at the mention of Maud's name.

"She certainly did," said Mrs Fennel. "But on Wednesday your headmistress called back to request that we swap, so that our sports day is today and yours is tomorrow."

"The Head?" said Mr Galahad. "I can't see why she'd have done that without telling us.

Are you sure that's what she said?"

"Of course I'm sure," said Mrs Fennel. "I wrote it in my notebook, changed the date in my diary and even swapped the stickers on my wall planner. I don't just do things willy-nilly, you know."

While the teachers carried on with their argument, Maud thought about what she'd overheard in the Head's office the previous day. Hadn't she said something about a swap?

Out of the corner of her eye, she noticed someone smirking at her. Poisonous Penelope. And suddenly, it all made sense. Penelope must have pretended to be the Head! She must have called Mrs Fennel from the Head's phone, putting on the Head's voice, and requested that they swapped days. So when she came out of the office that day, and said she was talking to Maud's great-aunt about swapping classes, it was a total lie – the Head had never even been *in* the office!

*I knew she was up to something*, thought Maud. That witch was such a troublemaker! All she'd wanted to do was get all the Rotwood and Primrose Towers pupils together so that Maud might be exposed as a human.

"Well, it's too late for us to change our plans again," said Mrs Fennel, sharply. She pointed to a row of family cars that were pulling into the car park. "The parents of our pupils are arriving now, and several of them have had to miss very important meetings to come here on a weekday. One of them is a senior vice-executive, you know."

"The parents of our pupils are on their way too," said Mr Galahad. "And one of them is a Transylvanian countess."

Mrs Fennel seemed a little flustered by that. "Well, you may join in with our sports day if you like. If you think you can keep up, that is. We have a reputation for sporting excellence here. It might be a struggle for your lot."

Mr Galahad looked over at the bus, where Paprika was staring nervously out of the window. "You might be right," he admitted.

Maud couldn't believe what she was hearing. Obviously Paprika wasn't going to give the Primrose Towers girls anything to worry about, but some of the other Rotwood pupils, like Wilf and Warren, were very sporty. She looked over at Mr Von Bat, expecting him to stick up for Rotwood, but he was looking away from Mrs Fennel with a sheepish expression.

Several of the parents were lining up alongside the playing field now. Sure enough, Maud's dad was already wandering around with his travel flask, eagerly inspecting some of the other parents' cars. Her mum was sitting on her folding chair, waiting for the games to start.

A large black limousine pulled up in the car park and screeched to a halt, and a woman with flowing black hair wearing an ancient black ball gown stepped out.

Maud noticed Mr Von Bat give the woman a nod, and she frowned sternly back at him. At once Maud realised who it was – Paprika's mum! And from the look of her, it was no wonder Paprika was so anxious.

Maud glanced back at all the pupils on the buses. She didn't really want them anywhere near the Primrose Towers girls. It was true that if they didn't play, Paprika wouldn't have to impress his mum. But suddenly, Maud realised she *wanted* to play. Some of the students had been really looking forward to sports day, and there was no way Mrs Von Bat would be impressed if the Rotwood teachers backed down. They had to try, at least.

If Mr Von Bat and Mr Galahad weren't prepared to stand up for their school, it looked as if Maud would have to.

"We'll play!" said Maud to Mrs Fennel. "We'll take you on!"

She looked to Mr Galahad and Mr Von

Bat for support, but they didn't say anything. Penelope was staring at her, as if she couldn't believe Maud actually wanted to play the Primrose Towers girls.

"Won't we?" Maud asked.

"Um, yes," said Mr Galahad, closing the visor of his helmet. "Yes, I suppose we will."

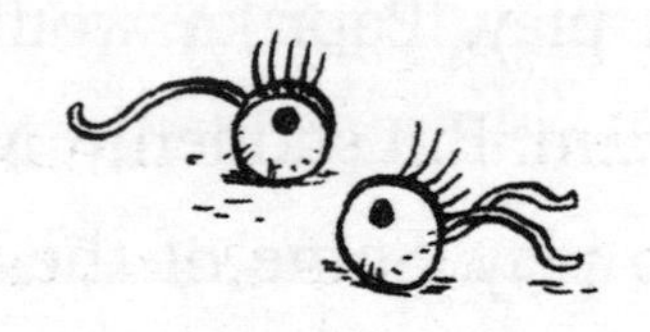

# Chapter Eleven

Maud yelled like a true monster.
"Come on, Paprika! You can do it!"

Paprika struggled across the finish line. Maud and Wilf applauded, but there was no one else around to join in. Only Paprika's mum was left at the side of the track, and she was so tired of waiting for him to finish that she was busy filing her nails into long, sharp points.

"I knew I'd come last," said Paprika, flopping to the ground and panting.

"At least you finished," said Maud. "Lots of people would have given up when all the spectators walked away."

Maud was beginning to regret encouraging Rotwood to join in with the Primrose Towers sports day. For a start, they'd all had to keep their coats, hats and scarves on for disguise, which wasn't helping with their athletic ability. Even worse, they weren't able to do their own Rotwood events and had to take part in the ones planned for the Primrose Towers girls instead!

Rotwood pupils had come last in all the sprint events, the sack race and even the skipping race, which was so sweet, most of the monsters couldn't even watch. It wasn't fair. Primrose Towers could at least have included some swamp-diving, or some grave-hopping or beetle-jousting to give them a chance. But Maud could hardly suggest that to Mrs Fennel.

Maud had been counting on Wilf's brother Warren at least to win a medal in the hundred-metres sprint, but he'd been distracted by a passing squirrel and run off in the wrong direction, barking loudly and scaring several of the Primrose Towers parents.

The only Rotwood pupil who had won anything was Penelope, who'd come first in the egg-and-spoon race. But Maud had seen her casting a spell to stick the egg and spoon together, so that didn't really count.

Maud and Paprika wandered back to the space behind the school buses where the Rotwood pupils were gathered. It was the only place they could be out of sight of all the humans, so they could fix their disguises and get treated by the school nurse, Mr Quasimodo's wife, a seven-foot ogre named Samantha.

The nurse grunted and took a moment to wipe the sweat from her green brow. It had been a very busy day for her. First she'd had to bandage up Martin, a mummy from Class 2C whose wrapping had come undone during the three-legged race. Then a demon from 4C called Roger had tripped over his tail in the backwards-running race and bruised one of his wings. Now she was sewing Frank Stein's hand back on after it had fallen off in the tug of war.

"You must tell your father to sew your body parts more carefully," said Mr Galahad to Frank. "It's no use him boasting about how he's created human life in his lab if he doesn't pay attention to detail."

"This hasn't exactly been monstrous for us," Maud said to Paprika. "We've only won one medal so far."

"I should have won one," said a voice that must have been Invisible Isabel. "I came first in the high jump, but nobody even noticed."

"Gather round, children," announced Mrs Fennel on her megaphone. "The final and most important event is about to commence."

*Oh well*, thought Maud, *at least there's one last chance for Rotwood to win a medal.* Although, whoever won, it definitely wouldn't be Paprika. As she walked back across the playing fields, she spotted Mrs Von Bat glaring angrily at her son from the crowd. It looked as if he was going to be in serious trouble when he got home.

The pupils gathered in front of Mrs Fennel as she lifted her megaphone again. "I'm sure you'll all agree that we've had a wonderful day. I'd particularly like to congratulate my little Primrose petals for winning all the medals." She had clearly forgotten about Poisonous Penelope's egg-and-spoon triumph.

"Three cheers for Primrose Towers," shouted Milly.

"Hip-hip, hooray!" shouted all the Primrose Towers girls.

"Three howls for Rotwood," yelled Maud, but the monsters were all too exhausted and disappointed to join in.

"Now to our final event," said Mrs Fennel. "And I'm sure you'll agree that this is the most exciting one of all – the obstacle course!"

The Primrose girls cheered again, and Mrs Fennel pointed to the far side of the playing field. There were nets, a line of balloons and a paddling pool with a wooden plank across it, and then the course continued into Primrose Woods, the trees to one side of the school.

For the first time that day, Maud thought things were starting to look up. Surely the Rotwood students could win this one? This course had no slime, no slugs and no snakes. There weren't even any hungry swamp beasts.

"I need three pupils from each school for this event," said Mrs Fennel. "Now gather round, Primrose petals, and I'll tell you who I've chosen."

As the Primrose Towers girls huddled around Mrs Fennel, the Rotwood pupils crowded around Mr Galahad to see which of them he'd pick. He considered them one by one, sometimes looking as if he was about to select someone, but then shaking his head and sighing.

"It might as well be you, Penelope," he said at last. "You're the only one who's won a medal so far. You can choose the others if you like."

"Thanks, Sir," said Penelope. "Let me see …"

Maud was convinced she'd choose Wilf and Warren. The Primrose Towers obstacle course didn't look as if it would be problem for either of them.

"I choose …" said Penelope, "… Maud and Paprika."

Wilf yelped with disappointment.

*Why has she chosen us?* Maud wondered. You could bet your eyeballs she hadn't picked her two least favourite classmates out of the goodness of her heart. She was planning something, for sure.

As Maud stepped up to the starting line of the obstacle course, she saw the three Primrose Towers pupils that Mrs Fennel had chosen: Suzie Singh, Amanda Derrington and, worst of all, Milly. Now she needed to win more than ever. She'd never hear the end of it if her twin sister beat her.

"On your marks …" bellowed Mrs Fennel, through her megaphone. "Get set … Go!"

The six pupils raced to the nets and got down on their hands and knees to crawl under them. As Maud struggled through hers, she saw that Penelope and all the Primrose Towers girls were already on to the balloons. Behind her, Paprika had got his cape tangled in the net and was still fumbling about underneath it. Maud considered waiting for him to keep him company, but she couldn't let the others get too far ahead. She couldn't let Penelope or Milly have the satisfaction of winning.

She raced to the pink balloons and stamped on them one by one. Next to her, Penelope hung back, eyeing the balloons suspiciously. They were covered in pictures of teddies, rainbows and fairy castles – no wonder the witch was hesitating. For a moment, Maud's heart leapt– this would slow Penelope down! – but the witch just waved her hand, and every single one of her balloons burst at once.

"That's not fair!" Maud cried.

"Diddums," Penelope replied, dashing off.

By the time Maud had finished popping her balloons and was tiptoeing across the plank over the paddling pool, Penelope and the Primrose Towers girls were racing off into the woods. Maud leapt off the end of the plank, desperate to keep up.

Unlike the gloomy forest surrounding Rotwood, Primrose Wood was light and open, with tall pines and oak trees dotted around gentle slopes, and bright glades filled with bluebells and foxgloves.

Penelope was inching ahead of everyone now. She looked back, as if checking that they were out of sight of the teachers. She reached into the pocket of her dress, took out a handful of bright red seeds and threw them behind her.

Maud recognised those seeds – they were from the Rotwood greenhouse! As soon as the seeds hit the ground, a tangle of green vines exploded up from them, and an angry red flower opened and chomped at the air.

Suzie Singh was heading right towards it. She tried to swerve out of the way, but it was no use. The jaws of the flower snapped shut around her ankle, tripping her up. She screamed and flailed her arms and legs about, but the plant held fast. There was no way she was getting free from that for a good while; she was out of the race.

Now Maud understood why Penelope had

chosen her worst enemies to race alongside her. She was planning to humiliate them all!

Penelope careered in front of Amanda Derrington and dropped some small white seeds. Huge grey mushrooms with red splodges shot up from the ground, directly under Amanda. One lifted her up into the air and kept on growing until it was as tall as a tree, leaving her clinging desperately to the cap of the fungus and wailing as it swayed backwards and forwards.

Maud's sister raced on, trying to overtake Penelope, while Maud kept a safe distance. Seeing the Primrose Towers girl gaining on her, Penelope scattered large handfuls of yellow seeds behind her. Green plants that looked like school-dinner cabbages spread rapidly across the ground, completely blocking the path.

Milly stopped in front of the rancid greenery, holding her nose to protect herself from its eggy smell. Maud held her nose too, but waded through, hoping she wouldn't slip over into the stinky leaves.

As soon as Maud was through, she sped up again. Penelope had disappeared around a corner. Maud looked back and saw that Milly was still trapped behind the cabbage, stamping her feet with frustration.

*So it's between me and Penelope now*, Maud thought. That meant that whatever happened, Rotwood would win the medal. But it wouldn't mean anything if Penelope won it by cheating.

The next section of the obstacle course was a rope tied between two trees. Maud struggled up the ladder and began to swing along the rope, hand over hand. But Penelope wasn't ahead of her. Maud glanced down, and saw that the witch had ignored the rope, and was running off to the side of the course, towards a holly bush.

"You have to complete all the obstacles," shouted Maud. "It doesn't count if you just run to the end of the course."

"I'm not going to run," replied Penelope with a grin.

Penelope felt around underneath the bush and pulled something out. Maud couldn't believe it. It was her broomstick! Penelope must have stashed it there earlier. Not content with eliminating everyone else from the race with seeds stolen from Mr Quasimodo, she was now planning to fly through the rest of the woods.

Maud was so angry, she almost fell off the rope, but she forced herself to cling on and get to the end before climbing down. Even if Penelope was cheating, Maud wasn't going to follow her example. She leapt towards Penelope and caught up with her just as her broom was taking off. Maud grabbed the broom's bristles.

The stick shot up into the air, but Maud clung on. They swooped over a line of tyres, which they were supposed to be stepping through.

"Let go, you stupid Tutu," shouted Penelope. She veered from side to side to try and shake Maud off, but Maud held on tight with both hands. Penelope steered close to a row of pine trees, but Maud managed to swing out of the way of each one as it approached.

Penelope tried swooping low over holly bushes. Maud swung her feet up and wrapped them around the broomstick, close to where Penelope was sitting. This was proving to be even tougher than the Rotwood obstacle course!

And then, out in front of them, a tiny grey bunny rabbit hopped on to the path. It looked up at them, nose quivering.

Penelope let out a screech of fear and steered violently sideways. She smacked right into the branch of an oak tree, let go of the broom and somersaulted into a pool of mud. Maud let go of the driverless broom, just avoiding the mud and tumbling into a pile of leaves instead.

Maud stood up, brushing leaves from her hair, and looked around. Penelope was still flat on her back. Oh dear! Was she hurt?

Penelope groaned and stirred. "Penelope?" Maud asked, rushing over. "Are you all right?" She held out her hand.

Penelope's arm shot up, grabbed Maud and pulled her down into the mud. Maud scrabbled around, stood, then slipped over again. By the time she'd got up and steadied herself, Penelope had disappeared into the woods. Furious, Maud tried to chase after her. But it was no good. She didn't even know which direction to go in.

After running for a while, she spotted the course of tyres, and followed them until she got to the edge of the trees. She was gasping for breath, fighting the stitch in her stomach.

Maud finally reached the end of Primrose Woods. As she looked across the playing field her heart sank. Penelope was ahead of her, just a few feet from the end of the course. Parents of both schools were cheering.

Maud pushed herself on in a last desperate bid to win, but it was no use. Penelope crossed the finish line and threw her muddy arms into the air in celebration.

"I win! I win!" she shouted, pointing a dirty finger at Maud, as she struggled to the end of the course. "The medal is mine!"

But something didn't make sense. Among the cheering crowds, no one was looking at Maud or Penelope. They were focused on something else – or someone – just beyond the witch. A huge grin spread across Maud's face. "I wouldn't be too sure about that," she said.

Penelope turned round and let out a cry of horror. Lying flat on the ground with exhaustion … was Paprika.

Maud rushed over and lifted up one of the half-vampire's arms in triumph. While she and Penelope had been struggling with the broomstick, Paprika must have been finishing the course. He'd done it! The Rotwood pupils cheered even louder.

With what little breath she had left, Maud joined in.

# Chapter Twelve

Paprika blushed with pride as he stepped up to collect his gold medal from Mrs Fennel. All around him, Rotwood pupils were cheering and giving each other high-fives, except for Zombie Zak, who could only do a high-four because his index finger had fallen off.

Maud glanced over at Mrs Von Bat, who was standing at the sidelines. She didn't look happy, exactly, but at least she didn't look angry any more. That must have been pretty good by her standards.

The Rotwood pupils hoisted Paprika above

their heads in celebration. Penelope held up her egg-and-spoon medal and cheered for herself, but nobody paid her any attention.

Maud's sister Milly stumbled out of the forest at last, along with Suzie and Amanda, and headed straight for Mrs Fennel to protest.

"She trapped me with rotten cabbage!" sobbed Milly.

"She marooned me on a giant mushroom!" whined Amanda.

"A plant tried to eat me!" complained Suzie. "That cheating Rotwood girl is even more monstrous than Maud!"

Mrs Fennel raised a hand to make them stop. "Now, now, girls," she said. "That's not the Primrose Towers way. You must learn to accept defeat graciously. Though you wouldn't have to accept it at all if you spent more time training and less time making up silly stories."

Leaving them to their frantic protests, she turned to address the crowd again through her megaphone. "And now for our grand prize," she said. "As promised, the pupil who I believe has performed most exceptionally today will win a ride to Buttercup Farm on Prancer the Shetland pony. So let's have a round of applause for Farmer Gilbert and Prancer!"

A fat man with a quilted green jacket and long sideburns stepped through the crowd, leading an adorable chestnut pony that was so small it barely came up to his waist. The pony neighed and tossed its thick blond hair aside.

The Primrose Towers girls cooed with excitement when they saw Prancer, but the Rotwood pupils winced with fright.

"I can now reveal that the prize goes to …"

Mrs Fennel looked around while the Primrose Towers girls closed their eyes and crossed their fingers.

"… the winner of the obstacle course, Vladimir Paprika Wellington Counterweight Von Bat! I'm sure you'll all join me in giving him a round of applause."

The Primrose Towers girls tutted and folded their arms, while Paprika gulped with fear. In the background, Maud could just make out the familiar sound of Poisonous Penelope sniggering.

"Well done, lad," said Farmer Gilbert, leading the pony over to Paprika. "Step closer, she won't bite. She might give you a big snuggly kiss, though. She's a very affectionate creature."

Paprika inched towards Prancer, trembling.

Maud needed to act fast if she was going to save her friend from his horrible fate. She ran up to Mrs Fennel. "Excuse me, Miss," she said. "Could I borrow your megaphone?"

"I'm not sure about that," said Mrs Fennel, doubtfully.

"I promise I won't say anything bad."

"Hmm. Well, all right then." She handed it over. "Does your friend want to give an acceptance speech?"

"Um ... yes, something like that," said Maud.

Maud lifted up the megaphone and said, "Could I please have your attention for a minute?"

The Rotwood pupils and Primrose Towers girls turned to look at her.

"I'm sure you'll all agree that we've had a lovely day," said Maud.

"I haven't," said Milly. "Thanks to you Rotwood cheats."

"But let's remember that sports day isn't about winning or losing," said Maud, hastily. "It's about coming together and having a great time."

"And cheating, if you're from Rotwood!" muttered Suzie Singh.

"That's why I don't think the grand prize should go to the winner of the obstacle course," Maud carried on, doing her best to ignore the Primrose Towers girls.

"Oh, she's going to try and steal the prize for

herself," said Milly, rolling her eyes. "What a surprise!"

"I believe the prize should go to the unsung hero of the day," said Maud. "Without her, none of this would have been possible. This person had the idea of holding the Rotwood sports day at Primrose Towers in the first place. I'm talking, of course, about my friend, Penelope." Maud smiled sweetly as she handed the megaphone back to Mrs Fennel. Penelope went pale and shook her head – but Mrs Fennel didn't notice.

"Well," said the headmistress, sounding a little surprised. "That certainly is a lovely idea. "But what about poor Vladimir? We've already awarded him the prize."

"Oh, I don't mind," Paprika spoke up, turning to scamper away from Prancer. "I don't mind at all."

"Well, that settles it then," said Mrs Fennel. "The grand prize goes to Penelope!"

Maud, Paprika and Wilf burst into applause,

and the rest of the Rotwood pupils joined in.

"No, no, I can't accept this," said Penelope, backing away. "I don't deserve this."

"Oh, you deserve it," said Maud. "It's exactly what you deserve."

Farmer Gilbert guided the pony over, put a pink riding helmet on to Penelope's head and lifted her up. "Try not to struggle, lass," he said, as he settled her on the pony and fixed her feet into the stirrups. "You don't want to startle Prancer." He stood back. "There you go. Pretty as a picture. All the baby animals at Buttercup Farm are going to love you."

Penelope, too terrified to even mutter a spell, squealed with fear as Farmer Gilbert led her away on Prancer.

Maud went over to the side of the playing field to see her parents.

"That was a very kind thing you did for your friend Penelope," said Mrs Montague.

"I just had to," said Maud. "After everything she'd done."

"Well, it was very thoughtful," said Mr Montague.

A few feet away, Maud saw Paprika showing his medal to his mum.

"Well, Vladimir," she was saying. "That was mostly awful, but in that last race you were … not bad. Not bad at all."

It didn't sound like much of a compliment to Maud, but it must have meant a lot to Paprika because he was grinning so widely you could see his pointed fangs. Fortunately, no one else seemed to have noticed.

"I'm so glad you're happy at your new school," said Mrs Montague. "You never did enjoy being at Primrose Towers very much, did you? Rotwood seems like a wonderful place. Even if the pupils are a little … er … unusual."

"It's an absolute scream," said Maud.

In the distance, Penelope let out another screech of terror as Farmer Gilbert led her across the playing field and towards the farm, where all the adorable little piglets, foals and calves were waiting for her.

Other titles by A. B. Saddlewick:

ISBN: 978-1-78055-072-5

Available in August 2012:

*Freaky Sleepover*

ISBN: 978-1-78055-074-9

*School Scare*

ISBN: 978-1-78055-075-6